# The Mouse and the Elephant

Story by Narinder Dhami
Illustrated by Amy Schimler

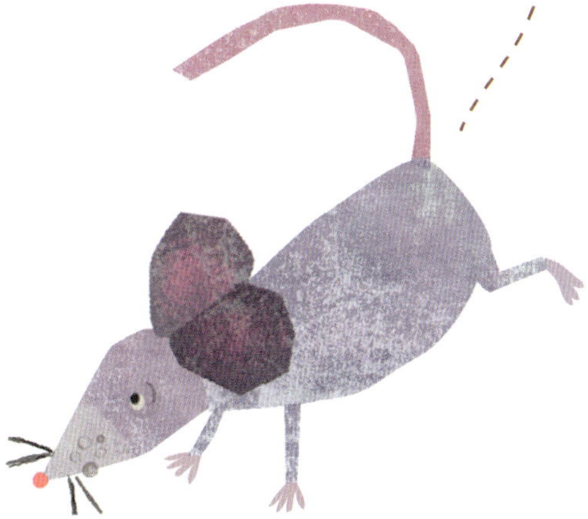

OXFORD
UNIVERSITY PRESS

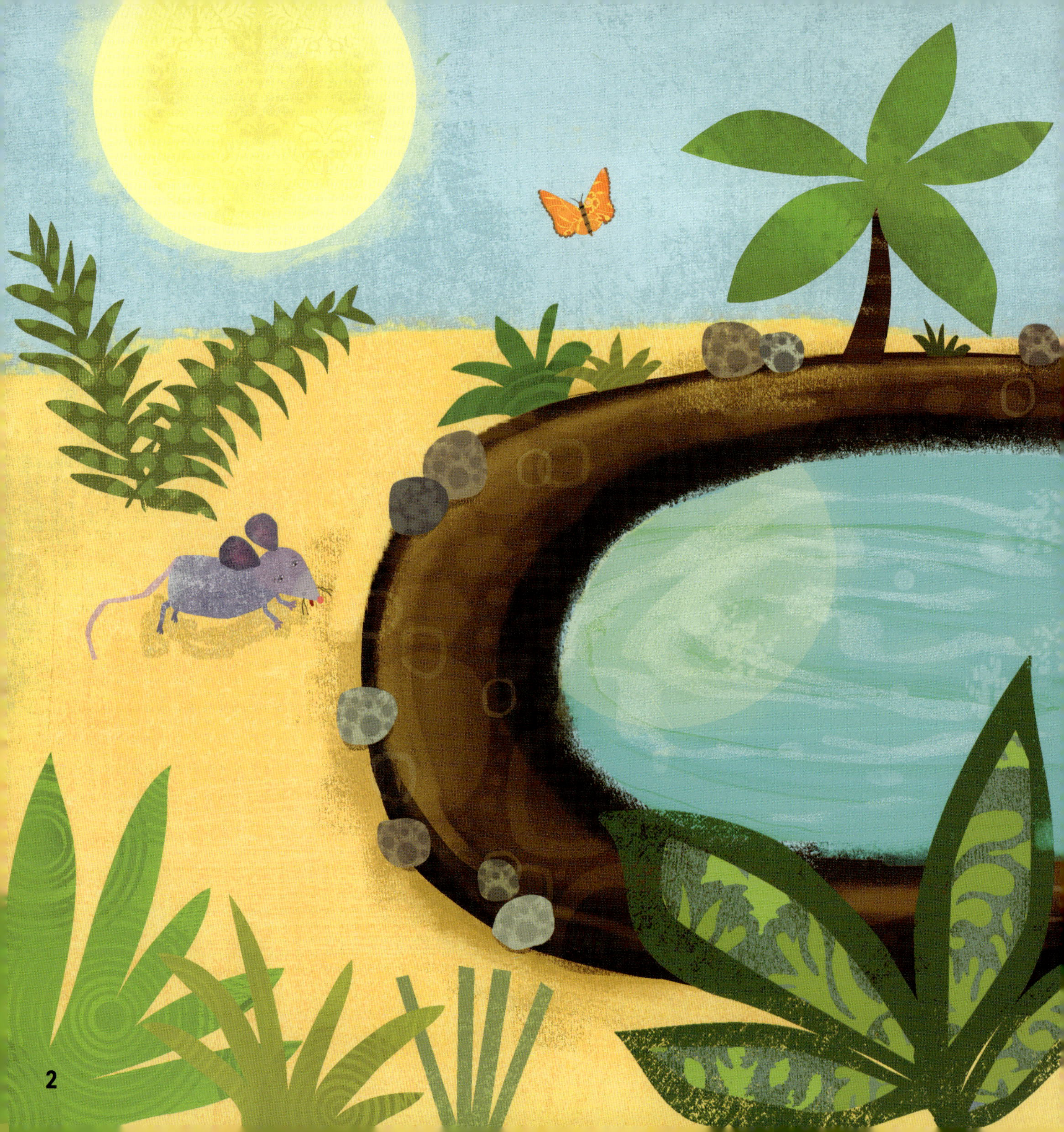

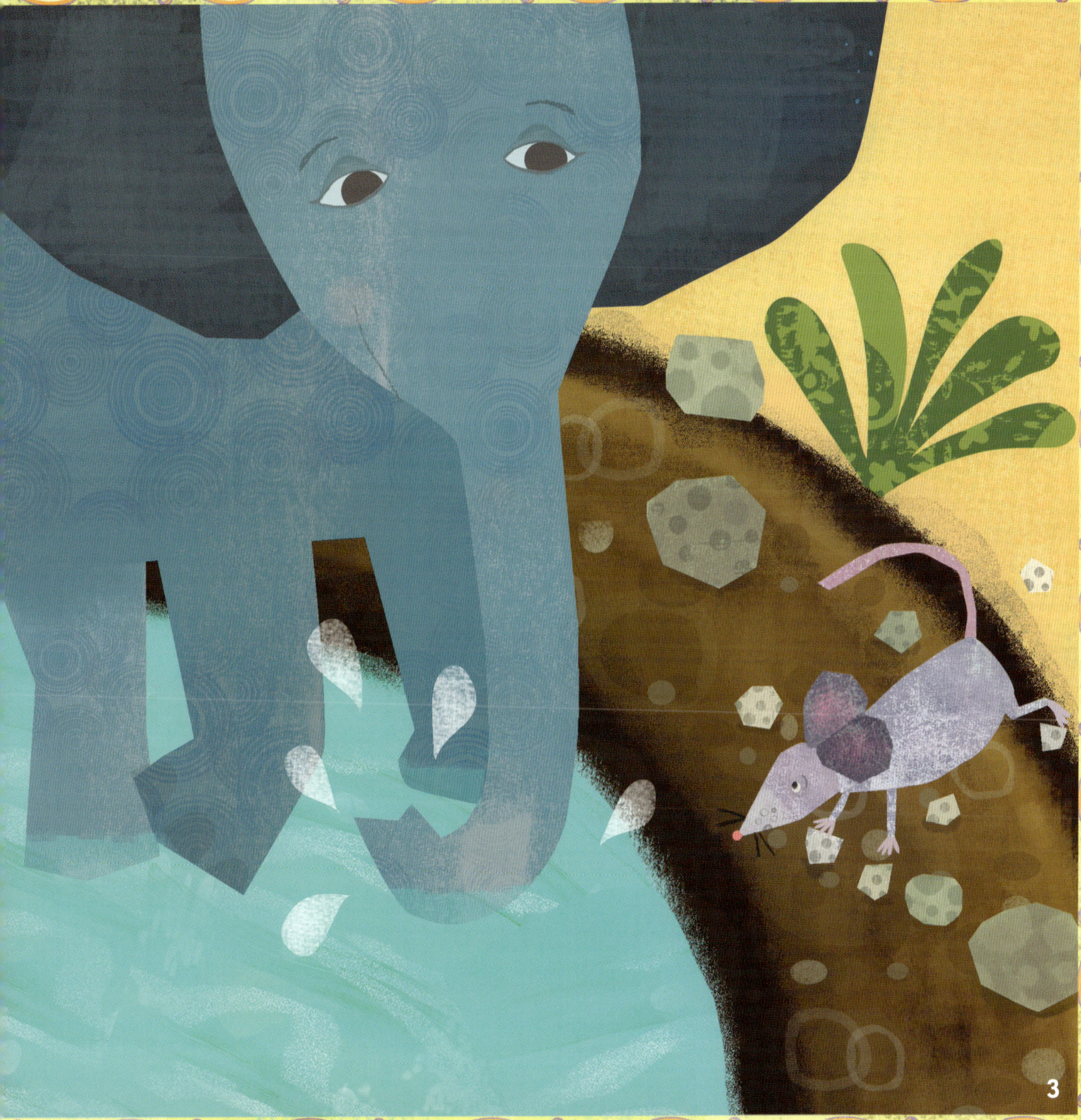

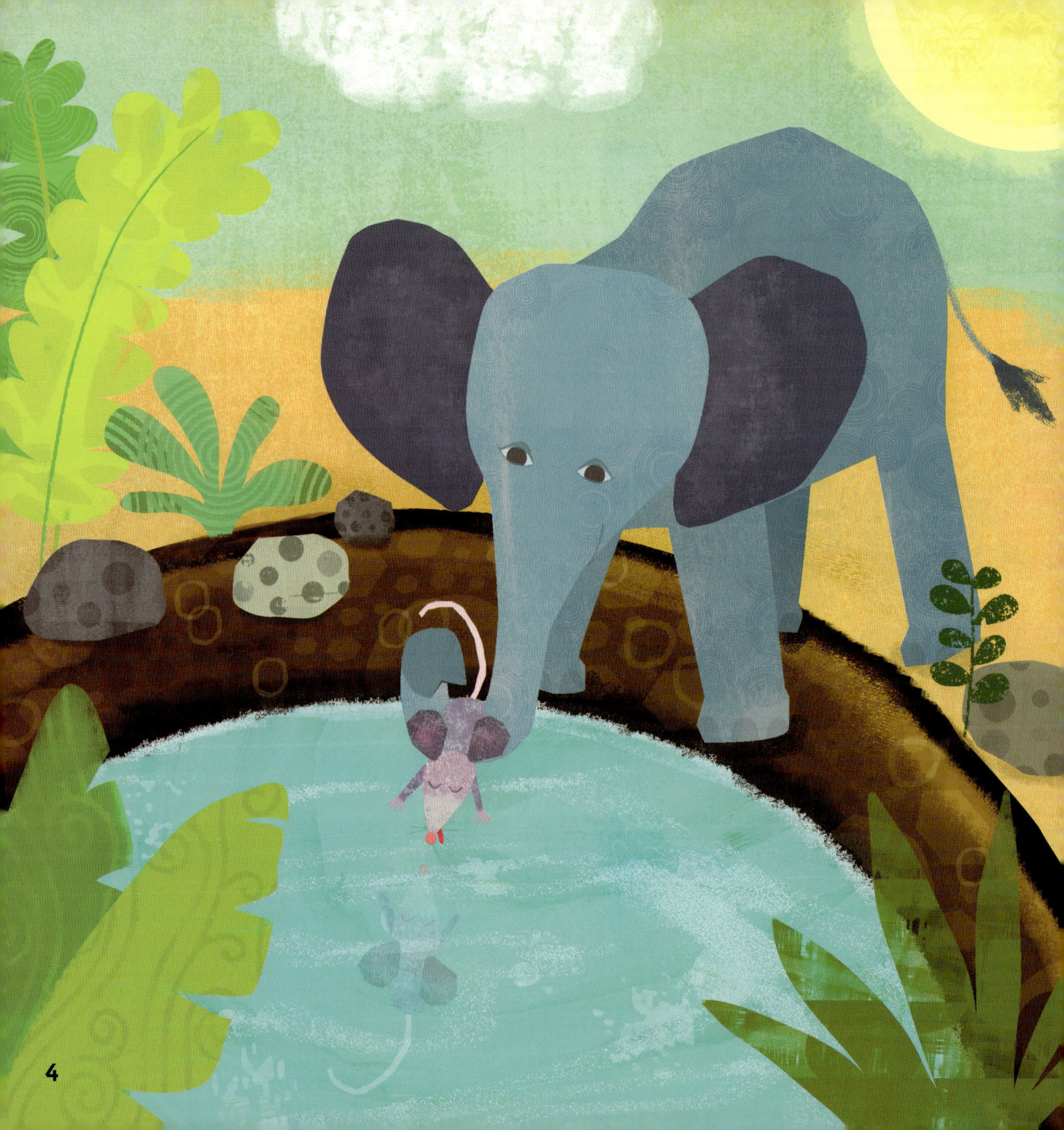

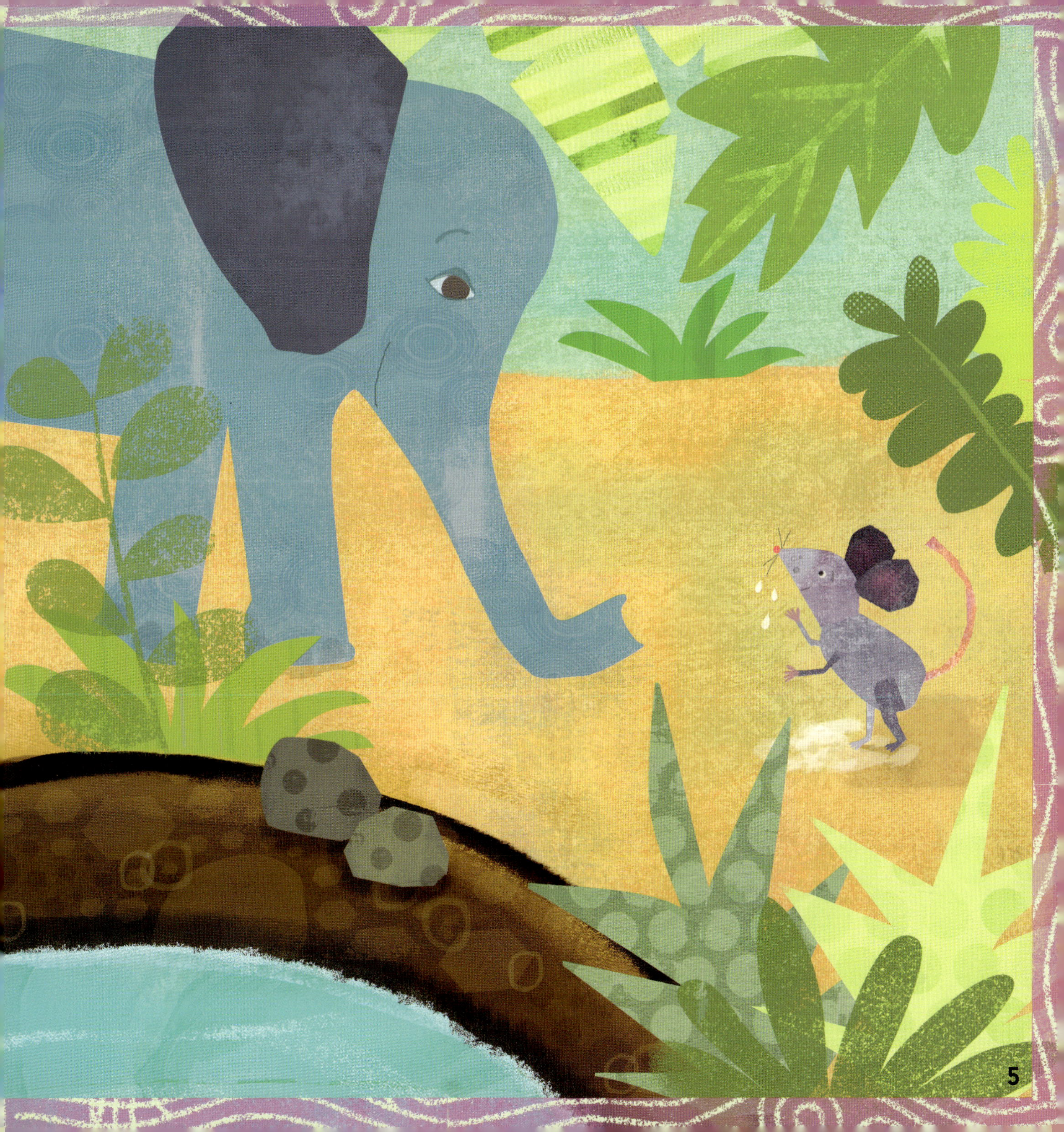

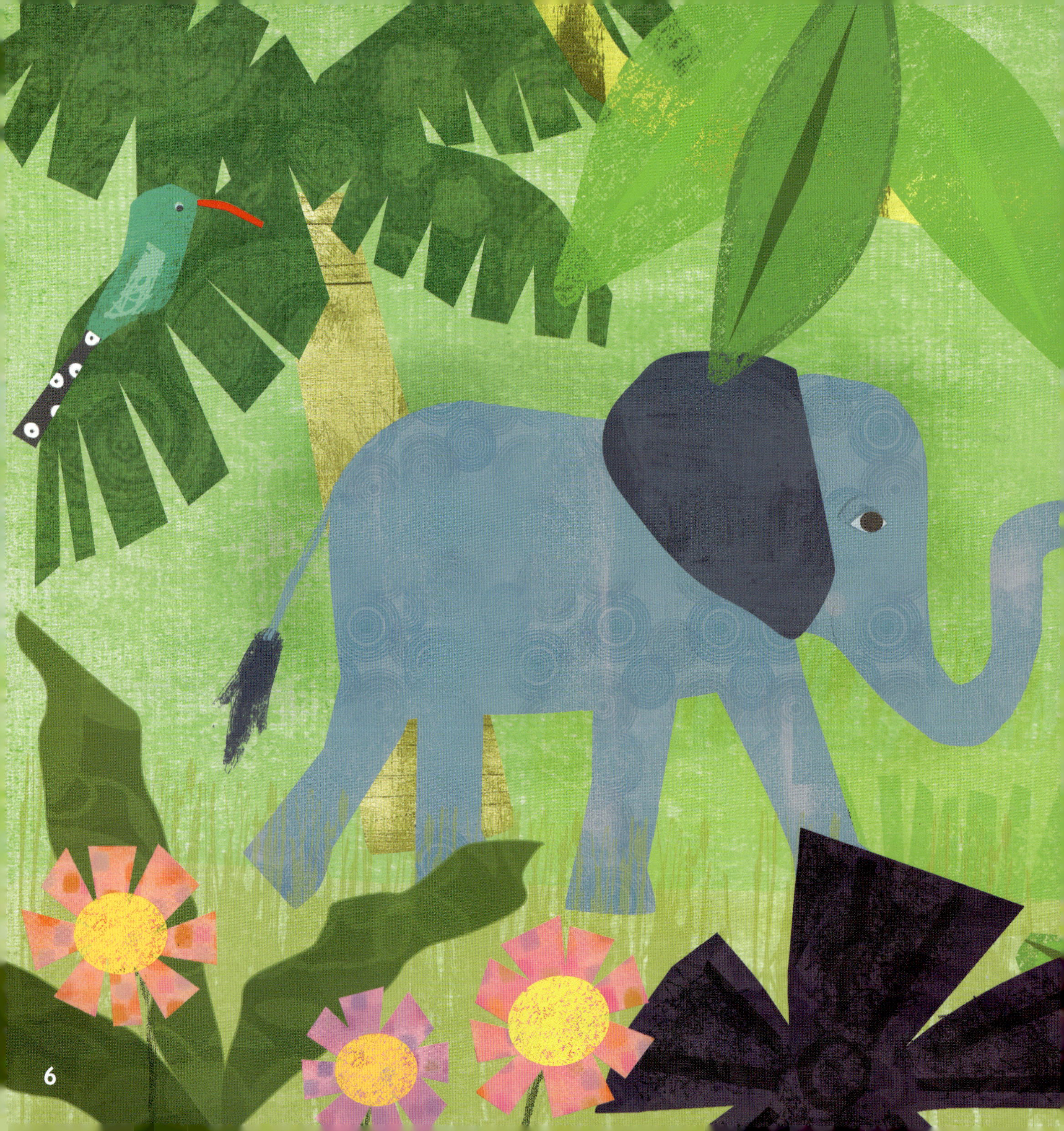

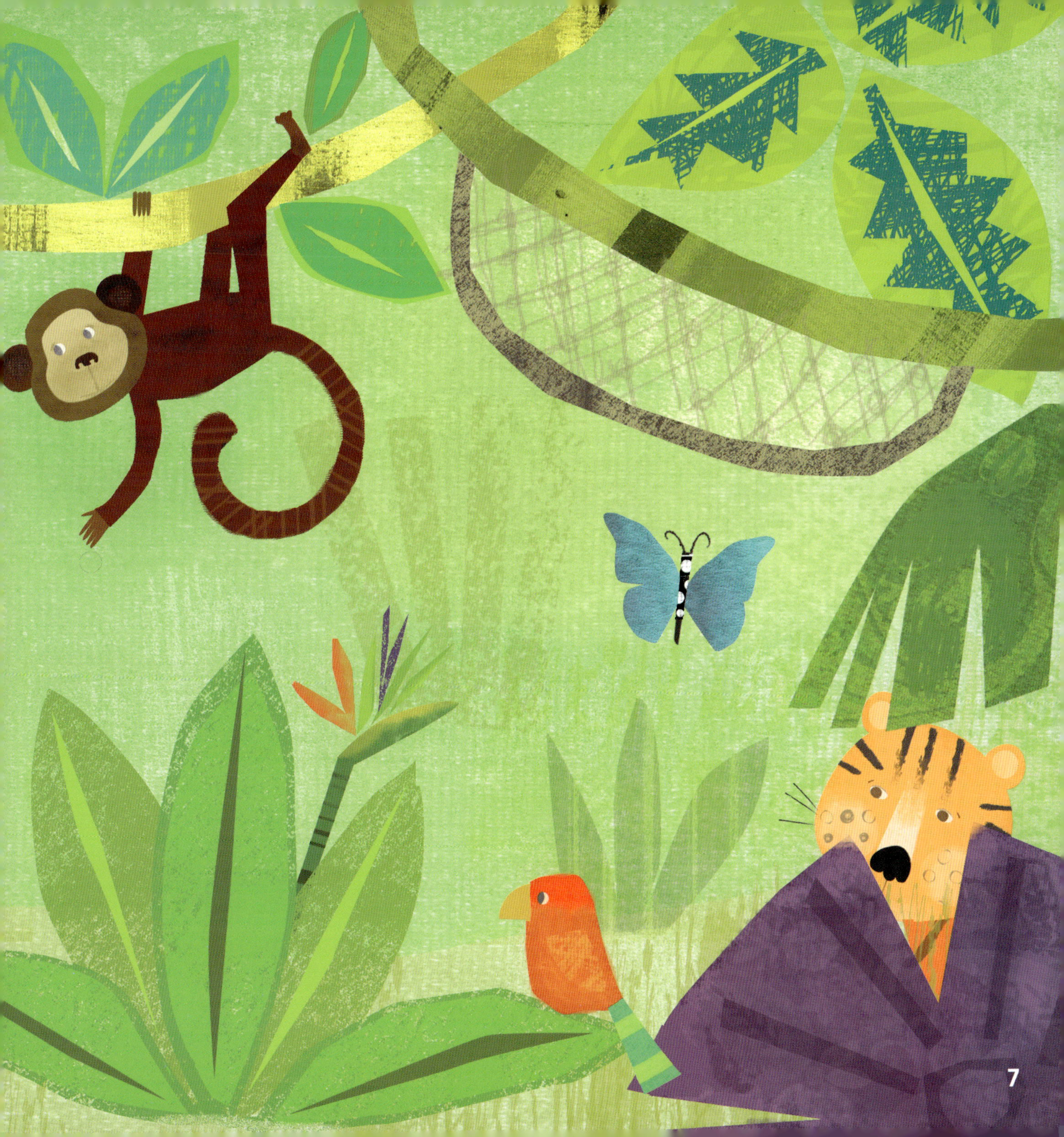

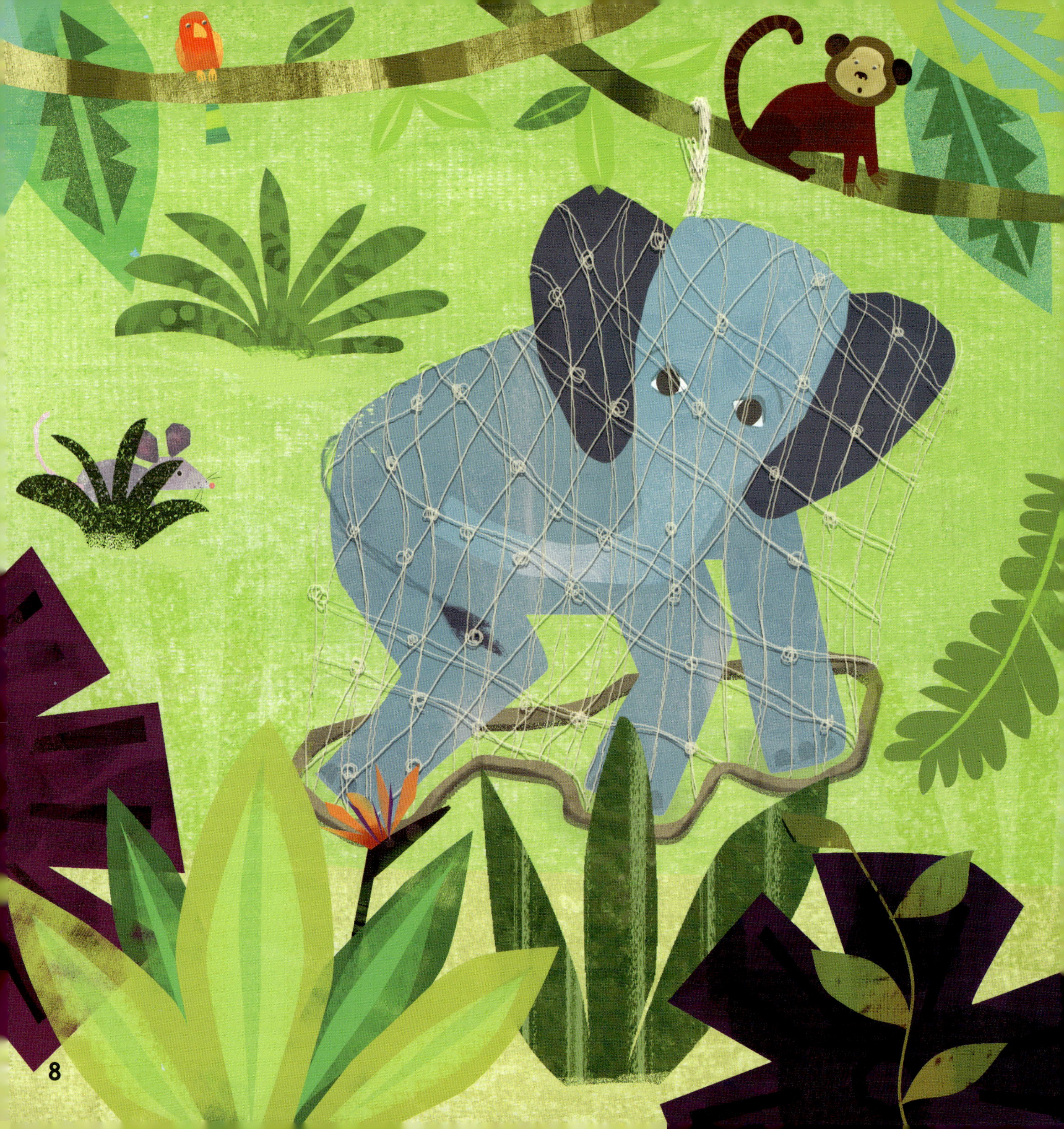

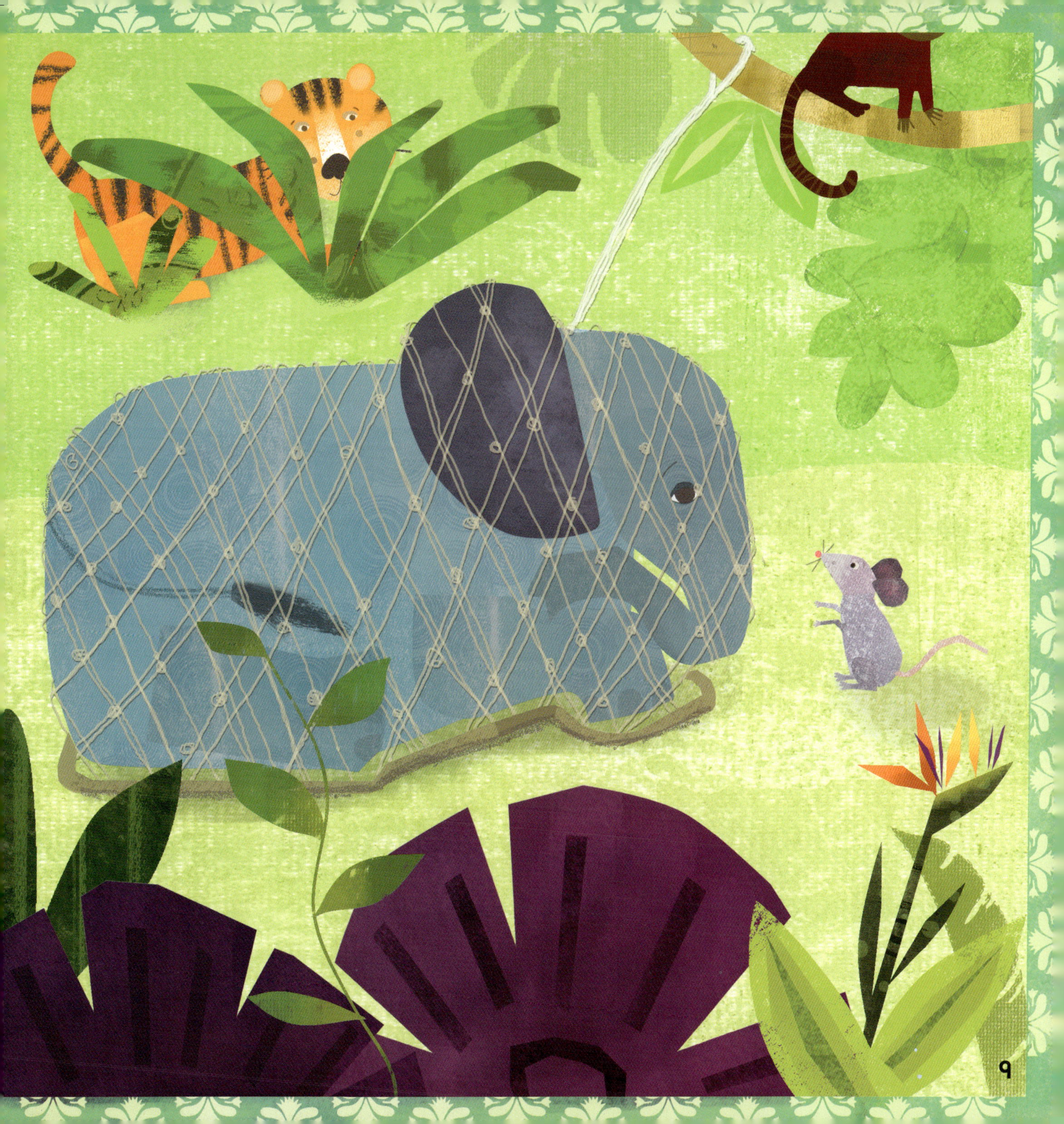

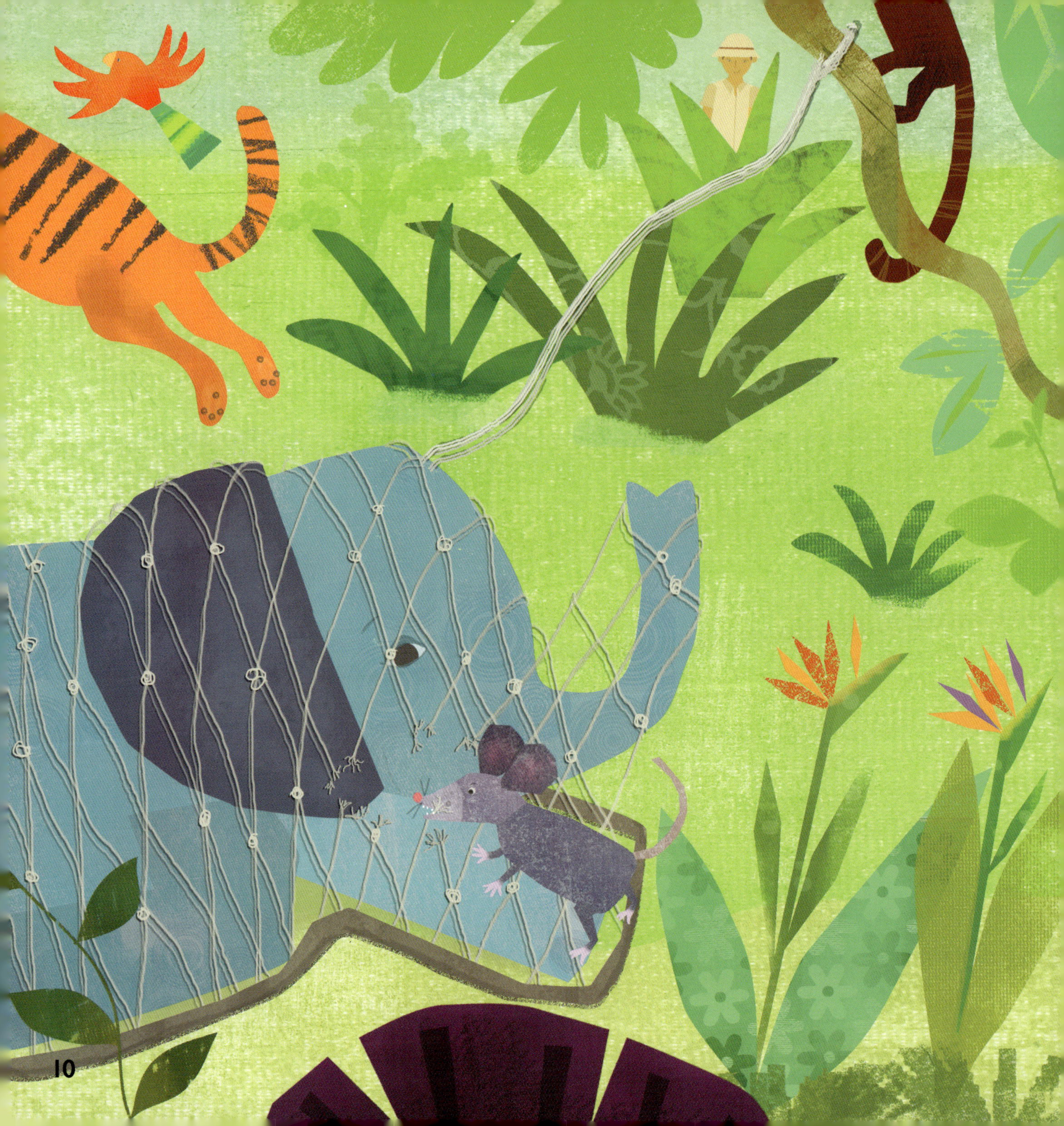

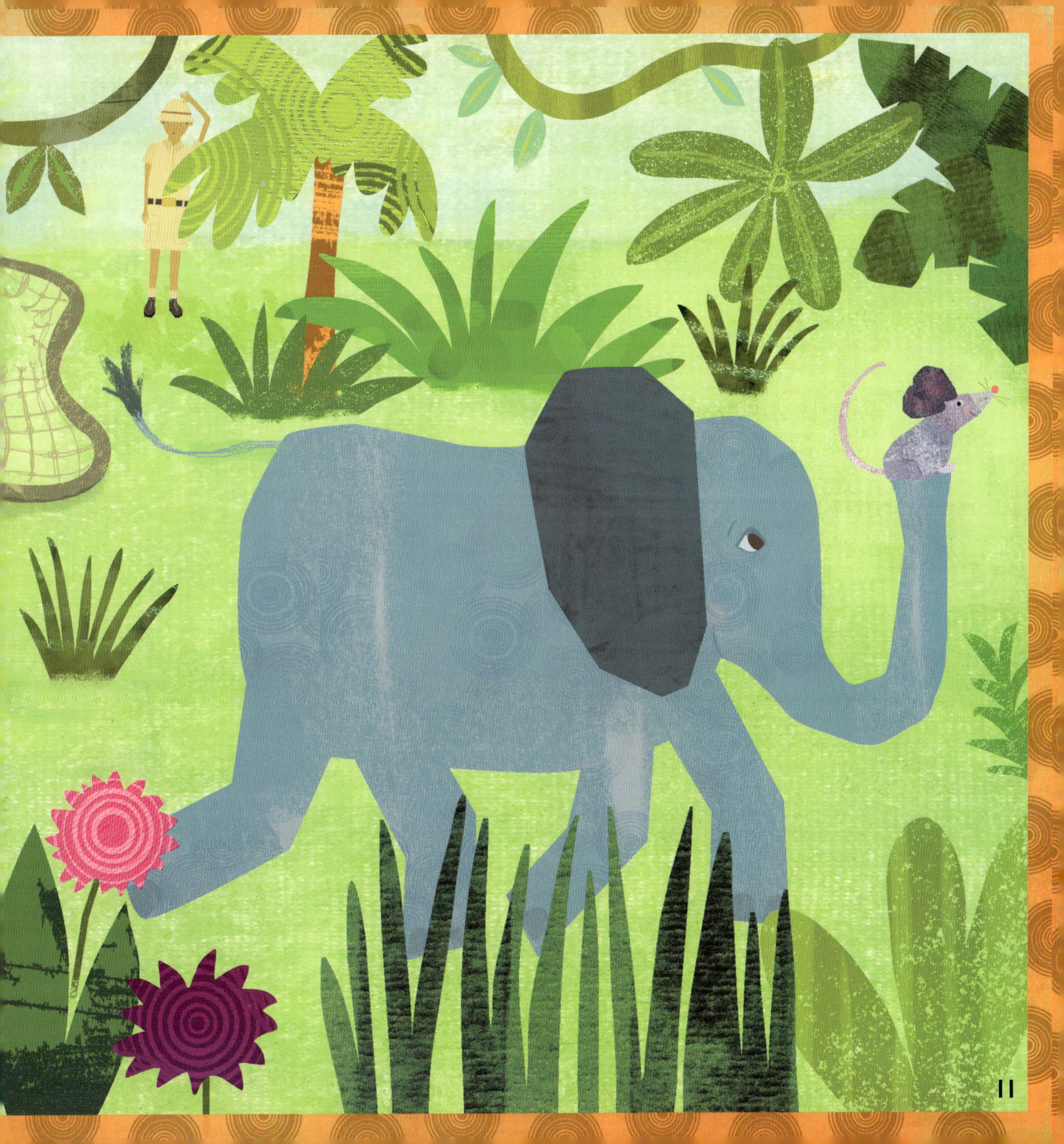

## Retell the story

**Once upon a time...**

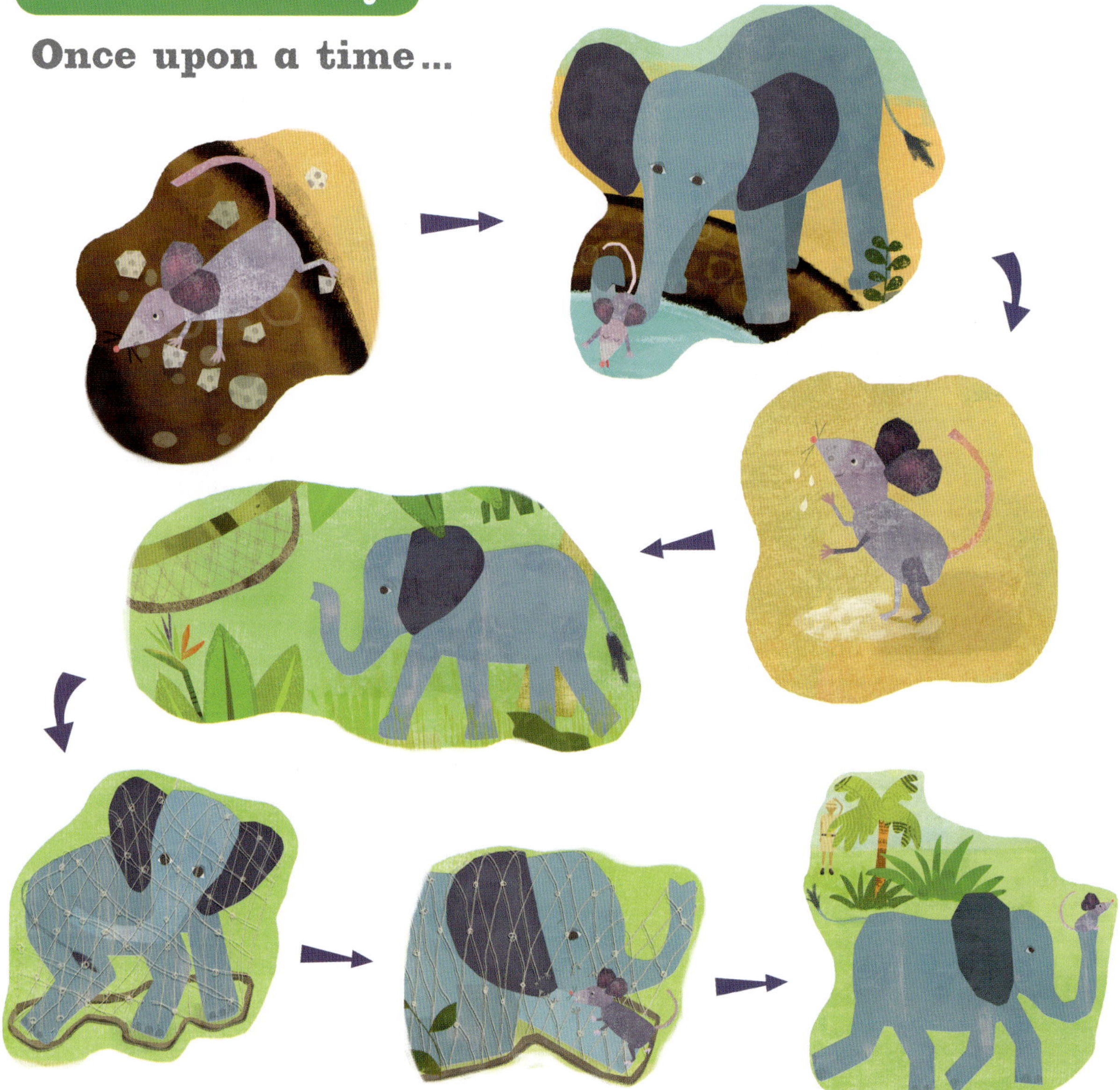

**The end.**